I GOT A CHICKEN FOR MY BIRTHDAY

LAURA GEHL
ILLUSTRATED BY SARAH HORNE

CAROLRHODA BOOKS
Minneapolis

For Loreen and Tom Gehl, who are just as fun and creative as Abuela Lola
—L.G.

For Iris
—S.H.

Text copyright © 2018 by Laura Gehl
Illustrations copyright © 2018 by Sarah Horne

Carolrhoda Books
A division of Lerner Publishing Group, Inc.
241 First Avenue North
Minneapolis, MN 55401 USA

For reading levels and more information, look up this title at www.lernerbooks.com.

Designed by Danielle Carnito.
Main body text set in Darling Nikki regular 33/38. Typeface provided by Chank.
The illustrations in this book were created in Indian ink with a dip pen. Color and texture finished in Photoshop.

Library of Congress Cataloging-in-Publication Data

Names: Gehl, Laura, author. | Horne, Sarah, 1979– illustrator.
Title: I got a chicken for my birthday / by Laura Gehl ; illustrated by Sarah Horne.
Description: Minneapolis : Carolrhoda Books, [2018] | Summary: A girl is disappointed when she receives a chicken as a birthday gift from her abuela, until she realizes the chicken is planning a bigger present for her special day.
Identifiers: LCCN 2017010270 (print) | LCCN 2017032200 (ebook) | ISBN 9781512498509 (eb pdf) |
    ISBN 9781512431308 (lb : alk. paper)
Subjects: | CYAC: Birthdays—Fiction. | Gifts—Fiction. | Chickens—Fiction. | Grandmothers—Fiction. | Hispanic Americans—Fiction.
Classification: LCC PZ7.G2588 (ebook) | LCC PZ7.G2588 Iag 2018 (print) | DDC [E]—dc23

LC record available at https://lccn.loc.gov/2017010270

Manufactured in the United States of America
1-41706-23520-7/24/2017

I *really* wanted tickets to the amusement park.

I told Abuela Lola three times . . .

I guess a chicken is better than socks.

Or a knitted sweater.

Or underwear.

Anyway . . .

I got a chicken for my birthday.

And now I have to feed it.

Well, at least I *do* love scrambled eggs.

WHISKING IT

HOW TO COOK EGGS

I got a chicken for my birthday.

And the chicken has a list.

SHOPPING LIST

- 100 STEEL GIRDERS
- 10,000 SCREWS
- 60,000 NAILS
- AN OLD LADY WHO SWALLOWED A FLY
- A HAMMER
- DIGGER
- 600 BALL BEARINGS
- 51 SPADES
- A SPIDER TO CATCH THE FLY
- 41 WOOD PANELS
- 600 BAGS OF CEMENT
- CEMENT MIXER
- PLYWOOD FLOORING
- A CARRIAGE
- A HORSE
- FIREWORKS
- STRAW, STICKS & BRICKS
- BUCKET
- 33 CRASH HELMETS
- A BIRD TO CATCH THE SPIDER
- G

BALLS

. SHEEP

. BEETROOT

. 6 BOWLING BALLS

. CAT TO CATCH THE BIRD

. 7 BUCKETS OF SAND

. A WINCH

. DOG TO CATCH THE CAT

. MARY

. MARY'S LITTLE LAMB

. 85 RUBBER DUCKS

. POLLY

. THE KETTLE

. TEA BAGS

. MILK

. POM-POMS

. A GOAT TO CATCH THE DOG

. 50 TINY HAMMERS

. A COW TO CATCH THE GOAT

. HARD HATS

. A BALL

. AN INTERESTING HAT

. 7 SWANS A SWIMMING

. 6 GEESE A LAYING

. 5 GOLDEN RINGS

. 4 CALLING BIRDS

. 3 FRENCH HENS

. 2 TURTLE DOVES

. AND A PARTRIDGE IN A PEAR TREE

OK?

The chicken also has a plan.

I got a chicken for my birthday.

And now the chicken stole my dog.

And even my hamster.

I got a chicken for my birthday.
And the chicken has a *lot* of friends.

The chicken also wants me to call Abuela Lola.

Tell her to pack her bags!

I got a chicken for my birthday.

And the chicken brought Abuela Lola for a visit!

I got a chicken for my birthday.

And the chicken is a genius.

I got a chicken for my birthday.

And it was the BEST. PRESENT. EVER.

Next year, I'm asking Abuela Lola for a trip to the moon!